Squash by Josh, b'gosh!

by

Joan Fitzgerald

Illustrated by Elizabeth Uhlig

MARBLE HOUSE EDITIONS

Published by Marble House Editions
96-09 66th Avenue (Suite 1D)
Rego Park, NY 11374
elizabeth.uhlig@yahoo.com
www.marble-house-editions.com

Library of Congress Cataloguing-in-Publication Data
Fitzgerald, Joan
Squash by Josh, b'Gosh!/ by Joan Fitzgerald

Summary: The story of a young boy whose enthusiasm for gardening yields a bumper crop of
squash so great that he must find a creative and meaningful way to distribute it.

ISBN 978-0-9815345-6-5
Library of Congress Catalog Card Number 2010921146

Printed in China

For Ryan, Andrew, and John Poplawski

Josh's parents were delighted with him. He was their only child, and was a wonderful boy. But they had to admit that he was somewhat peculiar.

Josh developed intense interests in the oddest things. Last year it was rocks. On family outings, Josh would fill up the car with all the rocks he could find and bring them home. It didn't matter if they were unusual or pretty, or if they contained fossils. They just had to be rocks! When he and his parents visited the beach, Josh swam briefly and then spent the afternoon scooping rocks off the sand and stuffing them into the trunk of the car. At the baseball field, he crawled behind the bleachers digging up rocks.

"But why rocks?" his parents asked.
"I like them," he would reply earnestly as he crammed some small ones into his pockets.

3

4

His entire room was full of rocks of all sizes, from pebbles to boulders. They were on the dresser, in the closet, under the bed, on the windowsills, piled in corners. There were rocks everywhere.

Every spring, Josh's father dug up a patch for a vegetable garden in the very small backyard. It was just large enough to hold six tomato plants. There would be enough tomatoes for salad and Josh could learn how things grew.

Hoping to take Josh's mind off the expanding rock collection, his dad asked him, "How would you like a little garden of your own? I could dig up a few more feet back there."

Josh looked at the overturned soil. "I want a *big* garden!" he stated.

His father laughed and dug up an area about two by four feet. "Is that big enough for you?"

Josh frowned. "Bigger!"

His father turned over more sod so that the space was four by six. He stood back, perspiring. "Now, that's large enough for anything you want to grow."

"I want it wider!" his son insisted.

Reluctantly, his father extended the area to five feet by seven feet. "And that's enough!" he said.

Josh knew that it was not large enough for his garden, but he decided to say nothing for the time being.

"What are you going to plant?" his dad asked. "Some corn? A few rows of beans?"
"I'm going to grow squash."
"Just squash?"
"Squash."

Josh was probably the only nine year-old in the world who adored squash! He always asked for it for holiday dinners. His favorite was squash baked with brown sugar and butter.

"Where do we get the squash plants?" Josh asked his father.
"We'll drive out to the garden store where I buy my tomatoes."

8

At Gulliver's Nursery, Josh discovered that the only varieties of squash they stocked were Zucchini, Acorn, and Crookneck. His father bought three of each kind for him.

"But that's not enough!" Josh protested. "I want *all* the kinds of squash there are!" Remembering the rocks cluttering the corners of their house, his father decided to humor him.

"Your Aunt Kim has a seed catalogue that you can borrow. Order a few packets of seeds from it."

Josh's aunt dropped the catalogue off the next day, and Josh turned excitedly to the squash section. His eyes widened when he saw all the listings for squash. It was even better than he had hoped! And the descriptions! "Richly flavored. Low in calories," Josh read out loud.

He wrote orders for Hubbard, Butternut, Buttercup, and Spaghetti squash. "Tender, tasty, excellent flavor and firmness." He ordered Tahiti Melon, Sweet Dumpling, and White Pattypan.

"Josh!" his mother asked. "What are you going to do with all that squash?"

"*Grow* it! I *love* it!"

He ordered Early Prolific Straightneck, Jumbo Pink Banana, Black Magic, Hybrid Aztec, and many others.

"Josh! That's going to be enough to feed the entire city!"

"I want more—I want—"

"NO! You have ordered enough! How are you going to pay for these seeds?"

"With my allowance. I've saved thirty dollars."

His mother sighed. She too remembered the rocks. "Give me the money, and I'll write a check," she said.

When the seed packages arrived, Josh went over the directions carefully. Then he planted the taller varieties in the back of the garden and the shorter ones in front. There wasn't room for even half of the seeds.

Josh got a shovel from the garage and worked hard to dig up more of the grass. The plot expanded to six feet by eleven feet.

His father exploded when he saw the garden. "What have you done to my lawn?"
"I need more room for squash," Josh told him.

Josh planted Hybrid Jackpot and Yellow Bush Scallop. Then he dug up more of the yard. The area was fifteen feet by sixteen feet, but it still wasn't big enough. Josh needed room for the Seneca Milano and the Sweet Mama. He dug up more.

Josh's father protested. "My whole yard is going to be full of squash!"

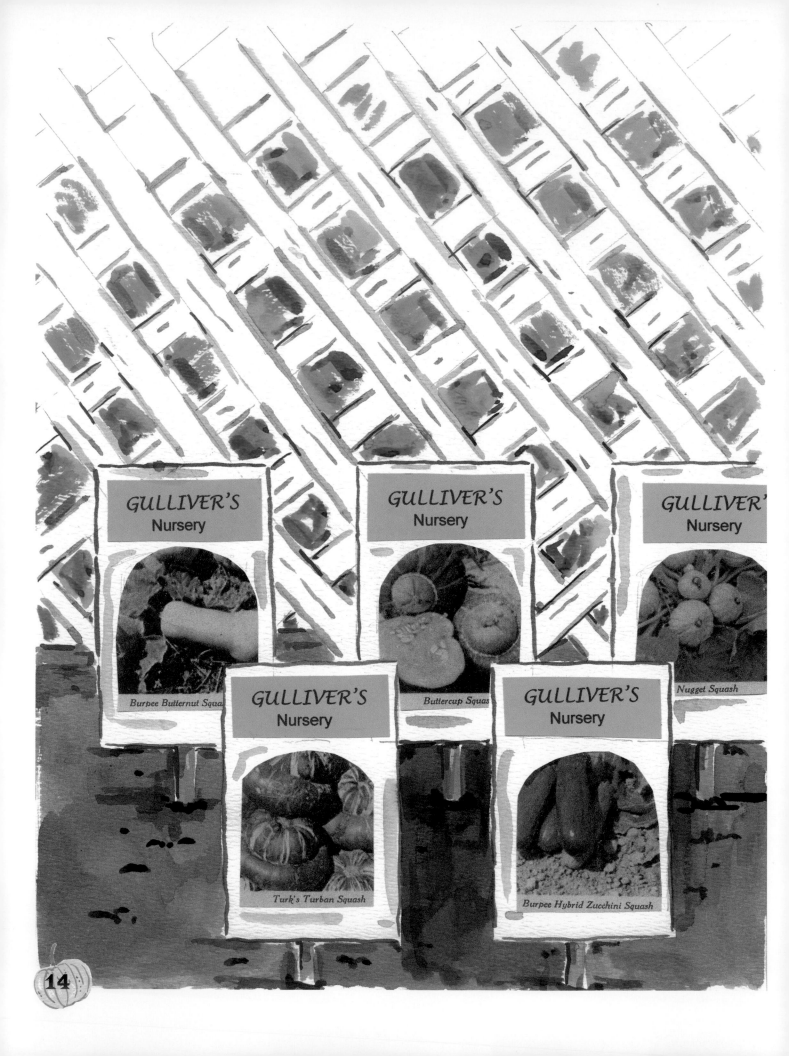

14

"Oh, leave him alone," his mother advised. "You can turn it back to grass next year. You're so busy this summer at work that you'll never have time to care for the yard. Besides, city gardening has become very popular."

Josh stopped digging up the lawn and instead dug small holes along forty-eight feet of the fence. There he planted Golden Dawn, Sundrop Hybrid, and others. He marked each one with a stake so that his father wouldn't mow down the tender plants.

Soon some of the squash started coming up and the vines grew rapidly. Josh watered them every day, and before long, they were spreading out over the yard in all directions. The fence was covered with lush, dense growth. Everywhere you looked, there were masses and masses of squash vines. Some of them started crawling on the roof of the house next door!

Then the vegetables appeared and the plants leaped eagerly into the yard. A few started to climb the sides of the house. Hanging near the eaves were vivid purple-topped White Globe. Around the foundation huddled huge, magnificent Blue Hubbard. Josh was amazed. He spent hours among the wonderful plants.

But when summer came and more plants ripened, there was a problem. Although Josh's mother served some of the squash each night for dinner and had filled up the freezer, there was no way the family could eat all that squash.

They gave baskets of squash to the neighbors, but soon they too had too much. "No, thank you," Mrs. Santiago said. "We still have some of the Zucchini you gave us last week."
"There are four Crooknecks in my refrigerator," Mr. Rogowski told Josh.
"My family simply will not eat another one," Anita next door said.

"I can't stand any more of this!" Josh's father said angrily one evening when yet *another* squash dish appeared on the table.

"Something must be done," his mother responded, noticing the incredible jungle covering their backyard. "We can't throw them away after all of Josh's hard work, but whatever can we do with them?"

A week later, Josh's mother noticed an article in the paper about local food pantries in town where homeless people could eat. They were asking for donations because their food supplies were lower than usual. More people had lost their jobs and the need was great.

"Here's the answer!" she told her husband, excitedly. "We'll take the squash to the food pantries!"

The Saturday News

Community Announcements

Still 25¢

Today's Weather: Fair and mild

LOCAL FOOD PANTRIES IN NEED OF HELP!

The Caring Place, a food pantry that supplies hot food for our town's homeless and needy population, has made it known that it has becoming increasingly difficult to provide balanced, nutritious meals. The Caring Place, which is run completely on donations, is appealing to the citizens of our community to offer money or food to this worthy cause.

All donations are welcome - fresh fruits and vegetables, canned goods, dry food (oatmeal, rice, bread), or a check in any amount. Anyone wishing to donate may stop in during business hours or call the manager, Ms. Reilly.

The Caring Place is located at 225 Orchard Street and their phone number is 755-4747.

GIANT BAZAAR PLANNED

The local Girl Scouts and ... town-wide bazaar to hel... learning project for cit... children will be eligib... farm this summer a... are raised and ca...

21

That Saturday, Josh helped his father load up the family car with boxes and boxes of squash. They drove to The Caring Place, a food pantry that served hundreds of people each day.

Josh was surprised when he saw the lines of people waiting outside the dining room. There were even kids his age.

The manager was very glad to see them arrive with their contribution. "We can serve summer squash with tomatoes this evening. Tomorrow, I'll bake zucchini bread, and I have a wonderful vegetable soup recipe that uses squash."

"Keep finding a lot of recipes," Josh's father told him, "because we'll be back next week with another carload."

All the rest of the summer, Josh and his parents brought squash to The Caring Place. When the winter squash ripened, the manager created new recipes.

THE CARING PLACE
Daily Menu - Monday

Fruit Juice
Mixed Salad
Rolls and Butter
Summer Squash Soup
Jello

THE CARING PLACE
Daily Menu - Tuesday

Fruit Juice
Fresh Celery & Radishes
Whole Wheat Bread and Butter
Zucchini Soufflé
Vanilla Ice Cream

THE CARING PLACE
Daily Menu - Wednesday

Fruit Juice
Cole Slaw
Corn Bread
Mixed Squash & Bean Stew
Rice Pudding

THE CARING PLACE
Daily Menu - Thursday

Fruit Juice
Green Bean Salad
Italian Bread and Butter
Spaghetti Squash & Tomato Sauce
Fruit Salad

THE CARING PLACE
Daily Menu - Friday

Fruit Juice
Assorted Pickles
Rye Bread and Butter
Fish Cakes and Squash
Cookies

WE WISH TO THANK OUR NEIGHBORS FOR THE GENEROUS GIFT OF SQUASH FROM THEIR GARDEN!

25

Josh felt good about his plants, but one night there was a frost and the vines turned black and died. He patiently pulled them all out and made an enormous compost pile.

"Well, Josh," his father commented, "are you going to grow squash next year? They certainly went to a good cause."

Josh thought earnestly. "I'm not sure," he answered.

Later that afternoon, as he rearranged the piles of rocks on the window-sill, Josh got an idea. *The Caring Place could use some brightening up*, he thought. *If every table had flowers on it, and the flowers were changed each week....*

"Mom! Dad! Tell Aunt Kim to get me a flower seed catalogue!" Josh said happily. "I am going to grow flowers *and* squash next summer. We'll dig up *all* the grass!"

The next year, Josh and his parents were back at The Caring Place with more cartons of vegetables, but this time they had an additional treat—bouquets of fresh zinnias, marigolds, and geraniums, to add an extra note of cheer to the dining room.

Josh was proud of his efforts and his parents were proud of him too.